# Mrs Potter's Pig

Phyllis Root

illustrated by

Russell Ayto

## WALKER BOOKS

AND SUBSIDIARIES

LONDON • BOSTON • SYDNEY

Mrs Potter kept a spotless house. The windows glistened. The floors glowed.

She even dusted the chickens until they squawked.

Everything
in Mrs Potter's
house was swept
and washed
and
polished
and mopped
perfectly
clean.

Everything except
baby Ermajean.
Ermajean
loved mess.

She drooled
and gurgled
on her white
ruffled dresses.

After every
meal, she had
apple sauce
behind her ears.

And any speck of dirt
in the garden clung to
baby Ermajean
like bees to clover.

"Ermajean," complained Mrs Potter,
"you're as dirty as a little pig.
Some day, if you're not careful,
you'll turn into one."

Ermajean even sounded like a pig.

She did not coo and babble like other babies.

She snorted and snuffled when she slept.

She gurgled and grunted while she ate.

One sunny day Mrs Potter tucked Ermajean into her pram, gave her a rice cake and wheeled her out into the garden to get some sun.

"Now sit here and stay clean," Mrs Potter told Ermajean. And off she went to dust the fence.

But Ermajean soon got bored.
Clutching her rice cake,
she crawled out of the pram
and across the lawn,
leaving a trail of crumbs
behind her.

Straight through the loose board in the
pigpen fence crawled baby Ermajean –
smack into the middle of the biggest, muddiest
puddle she could find. Ermajean squealed
with joy and dropped her rice cake in the mud.
A little piglet came and gobbled it up…

The piglet followed the trail
of rice cake crumbs
through the loose board
in the pigpen fence,
across the lawn and straight
up into the pram.

Mrs Potter dusted
the last stake in
the fence and stretched
her arms in the sun.
"What a fine day,"
she said to herself.
"I'll just take baby
Ermajean for a stroll
before I wax
the weather vane
on the barn."

She peered into the pram. Little snorts came from a bump under the blanket. How sweet, thought Mrs Potter, baby Ermajean is sleeping.

She wheeled the pram out through the gate and down the road.

"This road could do with some sweeping," she said to herself. The pram bounced and bumped and woke the piglet up. "*Snort,*" said the piglet under the blanket.

"The lilacs look
a bit dusty,"
Mrs Potter
remarked.
"*Snuffle,*" said
the piglet as it
hunted for more
rice cake crumbs.

"The trees could
do with a bit of
sprucing up,"
said Mrs Potter.
"*Grunt,*" said
the piglet. It poked
its snout up from
under the blanket.

She snatched the piglet out of the pram and hugged it tight. "Don't worry, Ermajean," she comforted the baby pig.

Back up the road she raced to call the doctor and see what could be done.

As she
opened the gate,
the piglet
squirmed free
and ran towards
the loose
board in the
pigpen fence.

"Come back,
Ermajean!"
Mrs Potter cried.
She sprinted
to the pigpen ...

… and there,
in the mud,
sat baby Ermajean.
"Oh, Ermajean, thank
goodness
you're
yourself
again!" cried
Mrs Potter.
"Come out of
there this instant!"

Ermajean squealed
and clutched
a fistful of mud.
"Come out right now!"
ordered Mrs Potter.
"Or I shall have to
come and get you."
Ermajean dug her
toes into the mud
and snorted
with glee.

Mrs Potter sighed. She took off her shoes and socks and climbed over the pigpen fence.

*Squooze* oozed the mud between her toes. "Oh," said Mrs Potter in surprise.

*Shloop* squelched the mud around her heels. "Why," said Mrs Potter, "this feels ... nice."

She squoozed and shlooped her way over to baby Ermajean, picked her up, and hugged her hard, mud and all.

"Ermajean," said Mrs Potter, "you are a pig. A happy little mud pig." Ermajean shrieked happily and plastered her mother's nose with mud. Right there in the pigpen Mrs Potter and Ermajean stamped and stomped and splashed.

Mrs Potter still keeps
a spotless house.
The doorknobs gleam.
The copper pots shine.
She even cleans the rubbish
before she throws it away.

But on sunny afternoons
Mrs Potter and
Ermajean slip away
to the pigpen ...

... take off
their shoes and dance
a messy mud jig
together.